W9-AJV-628

Dear Parent:

Congratulations! Your child is taking the first steps on an exciting journey. The destination? Independent reading!

STEP INTO READING® will help your child get there. The program offers five steps to reading success. Each step includes fun stories and colorful art. There are also Step into Reading Sticker Books, Step into Reading Math Readers, Step into Reading Phonics Readers, Step into Reading Write-In Readers, and Step into Reading Phonics Boxed Sets—a complete literacy program with something for every child.

Learning to Read, Step by Step!

Ready to Read **Preschool–Kindergarten**
• big type and easy words • rhyme and rhythm • picture clues
For children who know the alphabet and are eager to begin reading.

Reading with Help **Preschool–Grade 1**
• basic vocabulary • short sentences • simple stories
For children who recognize familiar words and sound out new words with help.

Reading on Your Own **Grades 1–3**
• engaging characters • easy-to-follow plots • popular topics
For children who are ready to read on their own.

Reading Paragraphs **Grades 2–3**
• challenging vocabulary • short paragraphs • exciting stories
For newly independent readers who read simple sentences with confidence.

Ready for Chapters **Grades 2–4**
• chapters • longer paragraphs • full-color art
For children who want to take the plunge into chapter books but still like colorful pictures.

STEP INTO READING® is designed to give every child a successful reading experience. The grade levels are only guides. Children can progress through the steps at their own speed, developing confidence in their reading, no matter what their grade.

Remember, a lifetime love of reading starts with a single step!

For Ella and Ava—K.L.D.
For SJ Kwon—J.A.

Published in the United States by Random House Children's Books, a division of Random House, Inc., 1745 Broadway, New York, NY 10019, and in Canada by Random House of Canada Limited, Toronto.

Step into Reading, Random House, and the Random House colophon are registered trademarks of Random House, Inc.

Visit us on the Web!
StepIntoReading.com
randomhouse.com/kids
www.barbie.com

ISBN 978-0-385-37304-3 (trade) — ISBN 978-0-375-97191-4 (lib. bdg.)

Educators and librarians, for a variety of teaching tools, visit us at RHTeachersLibrarians.com

Printed in the United States of America 10 9 8 7 6 5 4 3 2 1

Random House Children's Books supports the First Amendment and celebrates the right to read.

STEP INTO READING®

Barbie™ Little Lost Dolphin

By Kristen L. Depken
Illustrated by Jiyoung An

Random House New York

Barbie lives

by the ocean.

She loves
to swim!

Barbie also loves
to ride her Jet Ski.
She likes to go fast!

She rides
to a lagoon.
She hears a noise.
Squeak! Squeak!

It is a baby dolphin!

He is swimming

in the lagoon, too.

Barbie waves hello.
The dolphin is lost.
He cannot find
his family.

Barbie comforts
the baby dolphin.
She will help him
find his family!

Barbie gets
on her Jet Ski.

Barbie and the dolphin search all around the lagoon.

They see fish
and birds
and seaweed.
But they do not see
the dolphin's family.

It is getting dark.
The dolphin is sad.
Barbie has
to go home.

The dolphin does not

want her to go.

The baby dolphin
follows Barbie home!

Barbie calls
a dolphin expert.
She tells Barbie how
to care for the dolphin.

Barbie feeds
the dolphin
from a bottle.

Barbie sets up a tent.
She will watch
the dolphin.

Barbie pats him
on the head.
She says good night.

The baby dolphin
gets a good
night's sleep!

The next day,
Barbie's friends
come over.
The dolphin jumps!

He plays with them
and has fun!
But he misses
his family.

Barbie and her friends
will look for
the dolphin's family.
They ride Jet Skis.

The dolphin swims
next to them.
They look
near the lagoon.

They look

near a cove.

They cannot find
the dolphin's family!
They hear a noise.
Squeak! Squeak!

It is the baby
dolphin's family!
He could not find them.
But <u>they</u> found <u>him</u>!

The dolphins jump
and splash
and play.

Barbie and her friends watch the dolphin family play together.

Soon it is time
to go home.
The dolphins thank
Barbie for her help.

Barbie waves goodbye
to the baby dolphin.
She is so happy
to have a new friend!